HANNA'S
SABBATH DRESS

To Wendy Werner and to

Dr. Herman Gold.

Without their generosity and care,

this book would not

have seen light—neither would I.

—O. E.

HANNA'S SABBATH DRESS

AN ISRAELI FOLKTALE

by Itzhak Schweiger-Dmi'el

illustrated by Ora Eitan

translated by Razi Dmi'el, Ora Eitan,

and Philemon Sturges

Simon & Schuster Books for Young Readers

NEW YORK   LONDON   TORONTO   SYDNEY

There was once a little girl named Hanna.
Her mother made her a white Sabbath dress.
Hanna couldn't wait to wear it.

On the afternoon before the Sabbath, she took a
bath and then put on her new dress.

It was beautiful. Hanna was very happy.

Her mother was happy, too.

Then Hanna went outside.
Just past the gate her dog, Zuzi, ran up.
"Woof, woof," barked Zuzi.

"Look, Zuzi, look at the new Sabbath dress Mama made for me!" Zuzi wanted to jump up, but Hanna said, "No, no, Zuzi. You'll get my dress dirty."

She went a little farther and met Edna, the cow.
Hanna patted Edna and said, "Look, Edna, see the
new Sabbath dress Mama made for me!"

Edna bent down to lick Hanna, but Hanna said,
"No, no, Edna. You'll get my dress dirty."

She walked a little farther. Just as she turned around

to go back home, she saw a man coming out of the forest.

The man stopped and took a heavy sack off his back. Then he sat down to rest.

As Hanna came closer, she saw that he was an old man. He was covered with sweat.

She looked at him and asked, "Are you tired?"

"Yes," said the old man. "I've been in the forest since sunrise making charcoal."

"See my new dress?" asked Hanna. "It's my Sabbath dress. My mother made it for me."

"It's very nice," said the old man.

"Thank you."

The man sat a little longer and then he stood up.
"The sun has almost set," he said. "The Sabbath is
near and I must be on my way." Then he put the sack
of charcoal on his back and started off with slow,
heavy steps.

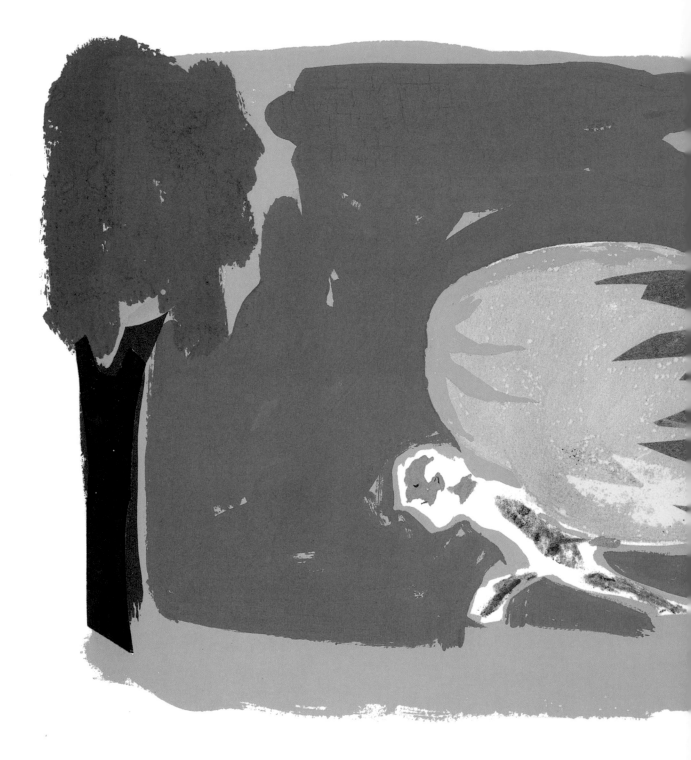

Hanna saw how his back bent under the load and ran up to him. "Can I help you?" she asked.

The man smiled. "That's very kind of you, little girl."

So Hanna walked behind him, with her arms stretched up high, to help hold up the heavy sack.

They walked along, talking together, for a while. Then the man stopped. "That's enough now," he said. "You're a good girl, but it's time you went home."

So Hanna turned and skipped happily down the
road until . . .

She looked down at her new Sabbath dress. *But
what is this?*

There was a black spot here, another there—and another.
Hanna's dress was covered with black stains from
the charcoal-maker's sack. The dress was ruined, and
on the very first day she wore it!

Hanna burst into tears.
When twilight fell, Hanna was
still sitting on a rock, all alone
in the field, sobbing bitterly.

The moon looked down and whispered in a voice that only Hanna could hear. "What happened, child? Why are you crying?"

Hanna could barely speak. She pointed to the black spots on her new dress. "Look, Moon," she sobbed, "my Sabbath dress!"

The moon looked. And then he asked, in a voice that only Hanna could hear, "Are you sorry that you helped the old man?"

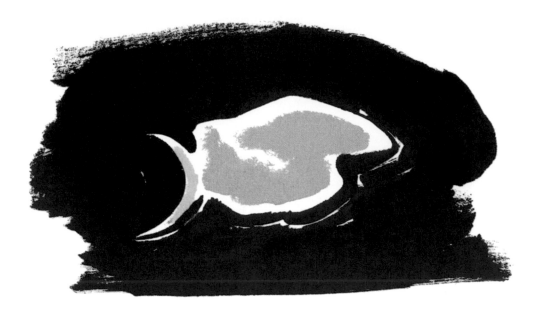

"Oh no, no. I'm not sorry at all. But the dress, my white Sabbath dress . . . my mother . . . "

Then the moon glowed brightly and whispered, "Don't cry, child. Go home now and don't worry about your dress. All will be well."

So Hanna started home.

As she walked along, the moon followed her. Moonbeams flooded down and touched the dress. Every black spot became a tiny bead of light. Soon Hanna's dress sparkled and glittered. It glowed like the purest silver.

On her way, she met her mother. "Who is this?" her mother asked.

"It's Hanna, Mama! Don't you recognize me?" Hanna laughed as she ran into her mother's arms.

As they walked home, Hanna told her mother everything that had happened.

Then they went inside.

And the whole room filled with light—the light of Hanna's Sabbath dress.

SIMON & SCHUSTER BOOKS FOR YOUNG READERS
An imprint of Simon & Schuster Children's Publishing Division
1230 Avenue of the Americas
New York, New York 10020
Text copyright © 1996 by Itzhak Schweiger-Dmi'el
Translation copyright © 1996 by Simon & Schuster
Illustrations copyright © 1996 by Ora Eitan
All rights reserved including the right of reproduction in whole or in part in any form.
Originally published by Le Maan Hayeled as "Simlat Ha'Shabat Shel Hannaleh" in
Kakha Sipru Li in 1937.
SIMON & SCHUSTER BOOKS FOR YOUNG READERS is a trademark of Simon & Schuster.
The text of this book is set in Italian Garamond
The illustrations are rendered in gouache
Manufactured in China
10 9 8 7 6 5 4 3
1014
Library of Congress Cataloging-in-Publication Data
Schweiger-Dmi'el, Itzhak.
       [Simlat ha'Shabat shel Hannaleh. English]
       Hanna's Sabbath Dress /
by Itzhak Schweiger-Dmi'el ;
illustrated by Ora Eitan.
       p.   cm.
       Summary: When Hanna helps an old man
and her new Sabbath dress gets dirty,
she is afraid her mother will be sad.
"Originally published as 'Simlat ha'Shabat shel
Hannaleh' . . . 1937"—T.p. verso
[1. Sabbath—Fiction. 2. Kindness—Fiction. 3.
Jews—Fiction.]   I. Eitan, Ora, 1940– ill.
II. Title. PZ7.S4123Han   1996   [E]—dc20
94-12819   CIP   AC
ISBN-13: 978-1-4169-7901-2
ISBN-10: 1-4169-7901-8
041526K1/B0608